HALLOWEENIES

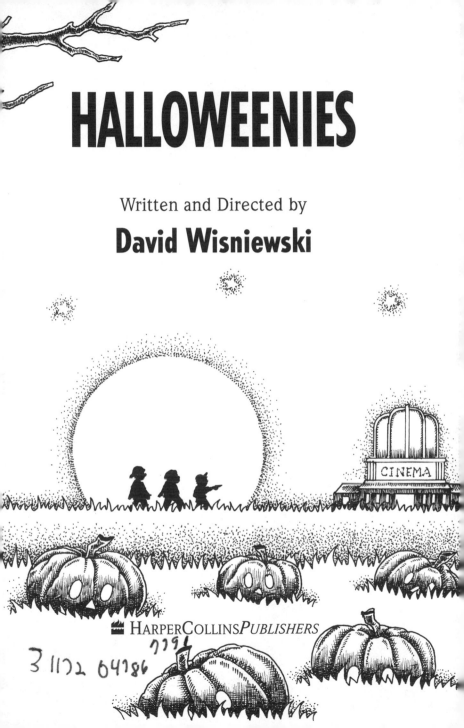

HALLOWEENIES

Written and Directed by

David Wisniewski

HarperCollinsPublishers

Library of Congress Cataloging-in-Publication Data
Wisniewski, David.
Halloweenies / written and directed by David Wisniewski.
    p.   cm.
    Contents: Curse of the werewuss—Frankenstein's hamster—Attack of the space toupees—
I forgot what you did last summer—The abominable showman.
    Summary: Five stories offer comical rewrites of well-known horror movies.
    ISBN 0-06-000513-0 — ISBN 0-06-000515-7 (pbk.)
    1. Children's stories, American.   2. Humorous stories, American.   [1. Humorous stories.
2. Short stories.] I. Title.
PZ7.W78036 Hal   2002   2001051640
[Fic]—dc21

Typography by Andrea Vandergrift
1   2   3   4   5   6   7   8   9   10
❖
First Edition

In memory of
<u>The Goon Show</u>,
for easy laughs
in hard times

OUR FEATURE PRESENTATIONS

K*a-BOOM!* Thunder cracked like giant knuckles.

Zizz-zizz-ZIK! Lightning poked the stormy sky like jagged fingers looking for change in the dark cushions of an angry couch.

Hairdresser Ramona Twinge drove through the deserted countryside in search of the Cleveland Cosmetology Institute. Wild boars and grizzly bears scrambled out of the way. Maybe I should've stayed on a road, she thought.

She consulted her map of Ohio. "Where am I?" she asked. As usual, the map said nothing. "You're a big help," said Ramona. "Maybe I should've bought a map of a friendlier state." The map stayed silent. "Yeah, you go ahead and sulk," she said.

Rain poured down like rain, only more so. Ramona shivered as the car filled with water. Maybe I should've rented a car with a roof, she thought.

A shark and an alligator jostled for space in the backseat. "You two stop fighting back there!" yelled Ramona. "Don't make me stop this car!"

"His knee touched my knee," said the alligator.

"I don't have knees," said the shark.

"I do," sneered the alligator.

The shark ate the alligator. "Now you don't," said the shark.

"That's better," said Ramona. "See how easy it is to get along?"

A sign loomed out of the darkness: BRIDGE OUT! Ahead, Ramona could see the swirling waters of a flooded river. Another sign appeared: BE BACK IN FIVE MINUTES!

"I can't wait five minutes!" fumed Ramona. "I'll be late getting lost!"

Then she saw the bridge eating a sandwich. It waved and offered her a cup of soup.

Three hours later, Ramona Twinge was lost on time. "Thank heaven!" She sighed.

Suddenly the car ran out of gas, oil, milk, and juice. The battery went dead, the tires blew out, and the engine started smoking even though it knew it was bad for it.

In the distance Ramona spied an old farmhouse. She knew it was old because there was a cow with a walker and a rooster wearing a wig. Ramona grabbed her suitcase of hairdressing supplies and trudged to the building.

A newspaper blew by her feet. WERE-WOLF EATS CAR FULL OF CIRCUS CLOWNS! the headline said. But Ramona's feet couldn't read, so she kept on walking.

A radio tumbled by. "THIS JUST IN!" shouted the announcer. "WEREWOLF EATS ELEMENTARY SCHOOL! PRINCIPAL CON-SIDERS EARLY DISMISSAL!" But a sound like the howling of a wolf was too loud for Ramona to hear the radio, so she kept on walking.

Then the Goodyear blimp sailed past. Electric letters twenty feet tall running all the way around it blinked. HEY, RAMONA! A WEREWOLF LIVES IN THE OLD FARM- HOUSE! But Ramona's attention was drawn to the huge hairy creature waving to her from the front porch. So she kept on walking.

"What terrible weather!" she said to the towering figure.

"Ruff!" snorted the beast.

"It is a rough night!" Ramona agreed. "I'm Ramona Twinge, a student at the Cleveland Cosmetology Institute. Pleased to meet you."

She shook the creature's paw. "RUFF!" it snorted again.

"Yes, it is," said Ramona. "Your hand feels like sandpaper. Let me give you a nice manicure!"

She went inside the old farmhouse. In the dim light, she could see clown shoes and rubber noses all over the floor. "Must have been a fun party," said Ramona. She sat down at one of the school desks piled against the wall and opened her suitcase. "Have a seat, handsome," she said.

An hour later the beast had polished pink fingernails. "I love that color on you," said Ramona. "Hmm! I bet your tootsies need attention, too." Another hour later the creature had pink toenails.

Ramona peered at the growling monster and bit her lip. "Don't take this the wrong way," she said, "but we've got to do something about your hair. It's not just the cut; it's the color."

"AROOO!" howled the beast.

"Well, whatever color 'aroo' is, it's not good. You need a complete makeover. Lean back and let Ramona work her magic."

Five hours later the beast was transformed. A perky wedge cut framed its horrible face. Blusher gave color to its swollen cheeks. Lip gloss added allure to its fang-filled mouth. Its shaggy fur had been shampooed, layered, and streaked with blond highlights.

Smiling, Ramona held up a mirror. "Get a load of you!" she squealed.

"AAARRGH!" roared the monster. "I'm no longer a werewolf! I've become . . . a WEREWUSS!"

Ramona's smile disappeared. "Well, thank you, too," she said.

The beast crashed through the wall and disappeared into the wilds of Cleveland. It was never seen or heard from again. Ramona shut her suitcase and trudged back to the car as the sun rose.

"I fixed the car," said the shark. "And I ate the map."

"That's just fine," said Ramona.

"How'd it go in there?" asked the shark.

"Some people have no taste," said Ramona.

Thunder rolled like a bowling ball inside a washing machine. Lightning lit the clouds like fireflies stuck in cotton candy. In the dark forest a crazed hermit stumbled out of his hut and glared madly at the author writing this story.

"Hey, *dummkopf*!" he shouted. "You started the last story this way!"

"Take it easy," replied the author. "You'll live longer."

"Don't tell me what to do, *schwein hund*!" screamed the hermit. "Change the beginning!"

"Have it your way," said the author.

In the dark forest a crazed hermit stumbled out of his hut, clutched his chest, and had a heart attack. "Aaarrgh!" he gurgled. "I should've kept my big Bavarian mouth shut!"

Meanwhile, on a bleak mountaintop, the castle of Baron Frankenstein scowled menacingly at the valley below.

"Sheesh!" said a palace. "What's up with him?"

"Oh, he's just mad," said another castle. "He's got an upset basement. You know, full of dungeons and laboratories and all sorts of evil. It can't help but show."

"Well, it really gets on your nerves," said the palace.

"Hey, Frankie!" yelled the other castle. "Do us a favor. Face the other way!"

Frankenstein's castle turned, bent over, and dropped its drawbridge.

"Oh, now that's just wonderful!" said the palace. "I could've gone all day without seeing that!"

Inside the castle Police Inspector Hans Tootle gripped his chair as the room spun

around. *"Ach du lieber!"* he cried. "What's going on?"

"The castle is unbalanced," said Baron Frankenstein, calmly picking a custard tart off the wall. "It's got a big buttress. Don't be concerned. It goes on a diet next week."

Inspector Tootle eyed his former enemy

suspiciously. The baron was a tall man with impressive bruises from low-flying aircraft. He had the same broad shoulders as his mother, a linebacker with the Oakland Raiders.

"Are you finished with my shoulders, dear?" asked his mother.

"Not yet," the baron replied. "I'll leave them in your locker."

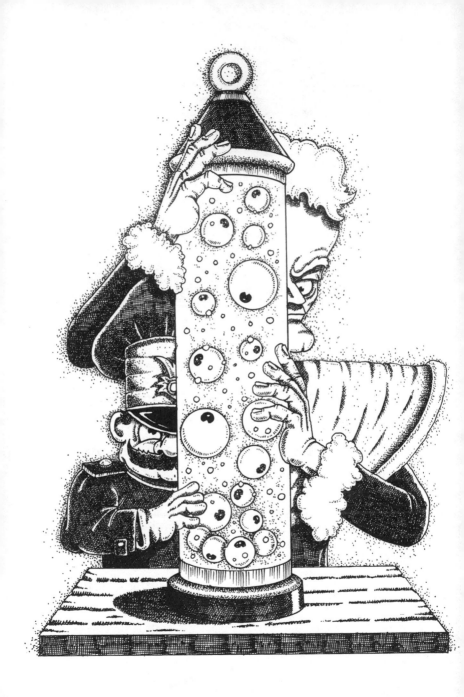

Inspector Tootle couldn't help but notice the baron's piercing blue eyes.

"You've noticed my eyes, haven't you?" Baron Frankenstein asked.

"Yes, I have," answered the inspector forthrightly.

"Aren't they beautiful?" queried the baron.

"Very beautiful," murmured the inspector.

Baron Frankenstein picked up the jar of piercing blue eyes and handed it to the inspector. "They're a gift from an old friend."

"How thoughtful," said Inspector Tootle. "Would this old friend be Igor, your half-insane lab assistant?

"Igor is now totally insane," the baron said icily. "He's worked very hard at it."

Tootle trembled with rage. "As hard as he worked with you to create a monster? A monster that did this to my arm?"

He rolled up the sleeve of his uniform,

revealing a bunny rabbit.

"And my leg?"

He rolled up his pant leg, revealing a dachshund.

"And my head?"

He tore off his hat, revealing a birdcage with two canaries.

The baron sighed. "The monster liked pets. He thought you would, too."

Tootle turned purple with fury. "NOT PERMANENTLY INSTALLED!" he screamed.

Baron Frankenstein waved his hand. "I'm sorry about your condition, Inspector," he said airily, "but there's nothing I can do about it."

The nose of Inspector Tootle's arm twitched maniacally. His leg growled. His head chirped. "You don't have to do anything, Baron," he said. "THEY WILL!"

Two fearsome figures entered the room. They were Igor and the Monster.

Baron Frankenstein turned pale. "What do they want?"

"They want to stay out of jail," said Inspector Tootle. "And I've given them the opportunity to do just that."

The Monster took a hamster out of its coat. Igor took an operating room out of his hat.

"Uh-oh," said the baron.

Back in the dark forest the crazed hermit opened his eyes and sat up. *"Himmel!"* he said. "I feel much better now." He looked up at the author. *"Dankeschön!"*

"No problem," said the author.

"What happened to the baron?" asked the hermit.

"Listen," the author said.

A terrible cry echoed through the valley. "GET THE SEWING KIT, MOTHER!" yelled Baron Frankenstein. "THE HAMSTER'S CHEWED ANOTHER HOLE IN MY PANTS!"

The alien spacecraft entered our galaxy without knocking. It hid in the bushes outside Pluto, then broke into our Solar System through a bathroom window. Jupiter thought he heard something but was too lazy to get out of orbit and check. The intruder crept through the darkness, then stopped. Someone had left the sun on.

The invader darted behind the moon, but more lights appeared. A comet flew by, followed by Donner and Blitzen and a fat man in a red suit. A better hiding place was necessary. While Mars watched Venus take a meteor shower, it dashed to Earth.

The ship's approach was undetectable except for twenty-seven massive explosions, a vapor trail that spelled "Eat at Orion's!," and a smell like cabbage being boiled with gym socks and tuna fish.

General Curtis Malaise awoke instantly. "Gracious!" he declared. "I'll never have pancakes for dinner again!"

At that moment the telephone rang. It was Private Driveway, the general's personal secretary. "General Malaise," he said, "an Unidentified Flying Object has been detected over Washington, D.C."

"Good heavens!" cried the general. "Has the President been told?"

"Yes, sir," said Private Driveway. "He thinks it might be Santa Claus."

"In July?" snorted the general. "Ridiculous! It's either the Easter Bunny or a big tooth fairy. Alert the troops! Scramble the jets!"

"Too late, sir!" interrupted Private Driveway. "The UFO has landed. You can probably see it from your front yard!"

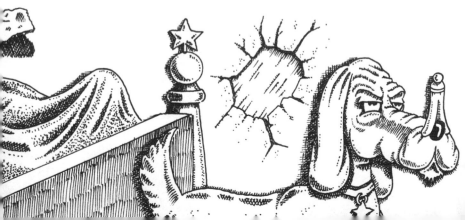

General Malaise put on his robe, opened the door, and stepped directly into the spacecraft parked outside. He looked around the vast empty chamber.

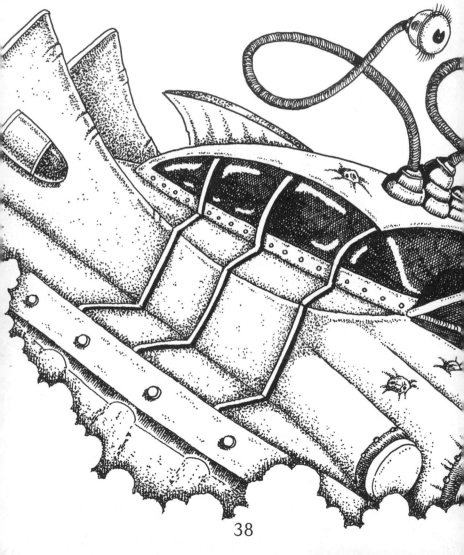

"Why, there's nothing out here at all,"
he muttered. "That private must be cracked.
However, the yard boy has done an excellent
job of raking the leaves. He even took the
trees."

Then something strange fell on the general's bald head. "Blasted pigeons!" he cried.
But when he reached up, his fingers touched
a mass of silky blond curls.

"Remarkable!" exclaimed the general.

40

"Perhaps those pancakes were worthwhile after all!" He hurried inside the house to examine his new hair. Behind him the alien ship jumped into hyperspace, stubbed its toe on the Washington Monument, and limped back into orbit.

General Malaise nodded approvingly at the golden tresses gleaming in the mirror. "What an improvement!" he exclaimed. "Except for the bifocals, hearing aids, and false teeth, I look like a teenager. A rather wrinkled teenager, perhaps, but still a teenager. Wait till the President and the Joint Chiefs get a look at me!"

Later that morning the President and the Joint Chiefs of Staff couldn't believe their eyes. "I must comment on how great Curtis looks today," said the President. "Where'd you get that hair, General?"

General Malaise smiled at his bald friends and proudly handed out his pancake recipe. Suddenly his locks leaped six feet in

the air, divided into sections, and flew onto the heads of everyone in the room. The alien hairpieces quickly overpowered the brains of their victims.

"Good work, Zontar," said the President, nodding stiffly. "How easy it is to control these Earth creatures! Like taking kloon-bang from a dingblorb."

The Joint Chiefs sat rigidly, then laughed in unison and gave a jerky thumbs-up.

"Thank you, Grebnek," said General Malaise. "Thank you, fellow krelnards!"

The attack of the space toupees had begun.

That afternoon, the First Lady had tea

with the wives of the military men. "They look like idiots," she said.

"I agree," said Mrs. Malaise. "And they walk as if their shorts were made of plywood. It's awful."

The marine commandant's wife raised her hand. "What's a krelnard? They call each other krelnards all the time."

"And they never blink," said the navy admiral's wife. "Brad didn't even blink when an anchor hit him in the eye. He just laughed and called me a dingblorb."

The First Lady cleared her throat. "Here's what I think," she said. "Their stupid blond hairdos are actually aliens from the UFO. They've taken over our husbands' minds and will use their positions of power to conquer the world."

"I think you're absolutely right," said Mrs. Malaise. "Men take so long to figure these things out. Now, what do we do?"

The First Lady held up a pair of scissors.

"It's time for a haircut."

The next morning the entire krelnard invasion force was in a garbage bag headed to the dump. The attack of the space toupees had ended.

"What happened?" gasped Grebnek. "Our plan was flawless!"

"We underestimated the females," wheezed Zontar. "Our mission has failed. We can only hope that the females of our species have more success."

High above Earth, the alien spacecraft prepared to unleash another wave of inter-galactic horror—THE INVASION OF THE SPACE GIRDLES!

Actress Buffy Gerbils turned to see a horrifying figure in the mirror. It was hers! "I've got more chins than a Chinese phone book," she pouted. "Now I'll never be in a Hollywood horror movie." She stamped her foot in frustration, then mailed it. "Great!" She sighed. "Now I'm fat with a limp!"

Suddenly there was a frantic knocking at the door. "Who's there?" asked Buffy.

"The Atlantic Ocean," said a strained voice.

Buffy raised a skeptical eyebrow. "How do I know you're the Atlantic Ocean?" she asked.

"Look through the peephole," urged the voice. "But hurry up! I gotta go!"

Buffy peered through the peephole. Sure enough, the hallway was filled with ocean waves. Buffy waved back. "Come on in!" she squealed.

The ocean poured into the room, soaking everything. "Oh, man!" said the Atlantic.

"This is so embarrassing!"

Buffy was about to get some paper towels when a fishing boat crashed through the doorway. On its shattered deck stood the terrifying figure of a crazed fisherman. Instead of a hand, he had four fingers and a thumb. And just below his knee was the lower part of his leg.

"ARRR!" he thundered. "DO YE KNOW WHAT YE DID LAST SUMMER?"

Buffy looked puzzled. "Not really," she replied.

"YOU DON'T?" yelled the fisherman.

Buffy shrugged her shoulders. "Nope!"

The fisherman's face reddened with embarrassment. "WELL, I WAS HOPIN' YE WOULD, 'CAUSE I CLEAN FORGOT!" He turned and sailed back down the hallway to the elevator.

"You can come back if you remember," called Buffy.

The crazed fisherman said nothing as his boat plunged down the elevator shaft. "Wait for me!" shouted the Atlantic Ocean. It paused on the way out. "Sorry about the carpet," it said.

The door closed quietly. Nothing remained to show what had happened except a plate of fried clams and a giant squid. Buffy Gerbils shook herself as if waking from a bad dream. "Oh, my!" she exclaimed. "Did that really happen?"

"Sure did," said the squid.

"Well," said Buffy, "now I can get back to complaining that I'll never be in a horror movie."

"You got that right," said the clams.

S ir Percy Fernwhipple inched his way up Mount Everest, then glanced back at the twenty thousand feet below. "Those feet smell terrible!" He gasped.

His Tibetan guide, Duk Pin Bo Ling, stopped to sniff the air. He screwed up his face. "We must stop now," he declared. "My face is screwed up!"

As Duk Pin arranged his features, Sir Percy let the cold white powder sift through his gloves. "What do your people call this?" he asked.

"My people call it snow," Duk Pin replied. "What do your people call it?"

"We call it the same thing," answered Sir Percy.

"What a stupid name for snow," said the guide.

"And this?" asked Sir Percy.

"We call it ice," said Duk Pin.

"How very interesting!" said the noble-man. "We call it . . . AIEEEEE!"

"That's a really stupid name for ice," said the guide. "Hey! Where'd you go?"

Sir Percy felt bad that he couldn't answer

right away, but he was busy falling to his doom. Three hundred feet below, a huge crevasse yawned. Then it rolled over, scratched itself, and went back to sleep.

The nobleman braced for impact against the jagged rocks. But at the last moment, a gust of wind broke his fall. "Thank heaven for breaking wind!" Sir Percy sighed.

When Duk Pin arrived later, he found the nobleman examining strange tracks in the snow. "What could have made these big footprints?" he asked.

"A Big Foot," replied the guide. "A creature my people call a yeti."

Sir Percy was intrigued. "Have you ever seen a yeti?" he asked.

"NOT YETI!" said a voice.

Duk Pin froze in his tracks. He chipped himself loose, grabbed Sir Percy, and scanned the slopes in alarm. "Did you say something just now?" he asked quietly.

"No," replied the nobleman.

"That's what I was afraid of," whispered Duk Pin. "Now, walk this way . . ."

"IF I WALKED THAT WAY," said a voice, "I'D NEED A DRESS!"

The guide's eyes widened in terror. "Climb, Sir Percy!" he yelled. "We must get back to camp!" The two adventurers clambered frantically over the icy rock. Behind them an ominous tapping echoed through the mountains.

Tippity-tappity, tap, tap . . . THUD!
Tippity-tappity, tap, tap . . . THUD!

"Sounds like a tap dancer," wheezed the nobleman. "Not a very good one, though!"

"It's the Abominable Showman!" gasped
Duk Pin. "It can't sing! It can't dance!"

"BUT I SPRITZ SELTZER DOWN YOUR
PANTS!" boomed the voice.

"Hurry, Sir Percy!" shouted the guide.

They pulled themselves into camp, stumbled into the tent, and zipped it shut. Outside the tapping grew louder. Duk Pin clapped his hand over the nobleman's mouth. "He's been performing the same dreadful show for centuries," he hissed. "Whatever he says, don't react!"

"WANNA THANK YOU ALL FOR COMIN' OUT TONIGHT!" a thick, raspy voice bellowed in the darkness. "ANYBODY HERE FROM PITTSBURGH? NAH, I DIDN'T THINK SO. HOW 'BOUT KAT-MANDU?"

Duk Pin and Sir Percy waited in tense silence.

"SHEESH!" said the voice. "IS THIS AN AUDIENCE OR AN OIL PAINTING? I'VE GOTTEN BETTER REACTIONS FROM FLU SHOTS. HEY! DID I TELL YOU I WENT TO THE DOCTOR? HE SAID I WAS TOO FAT. I SAID I WANTED A SECOND OPINION. HE SAID, 'OKAY, YOU'RE UGLY, TOO!'"

Sir Percy stifled a giggle. Duk Pin scrambled back from him in horror.

The voice drew closer. "HEY! YOU LIKE THAT ONE, EH? I GOT A MILLION OF

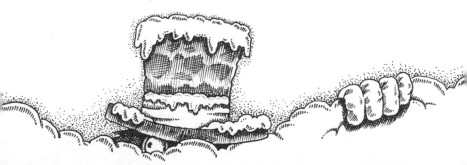

'EM. YA KNOW MY POOR DOG DOESN'T HAVE A NOSE?"

Sir Percy couldn't resist. "How does it smell?" he asked.

"TERRIBLE!" replied the Abominable Showman.

The nobleman guffawed. Duk Pin covered his head with a blanket. "Oh, come on, Duk Pin." Sir Percy laughed. "He's not that bad!"

The tent shook violently. "KNOCK! KNOCK!" said the Abominable Showman.

"Who's there?" shouted Sir Percy.

"LITTLE OLD LADY," replied the Abominable Showman.

"Little old lady who?" yelled Sir Percy.

"I DIDN'T KNOW YOU COULD YODEL!" roared the Abominable Showman. It ripped open the tent, grabbed Sir Percy, and disappeared into the swirling snow.

"Hee-hee-hee!" shrieked the nobleman. "You really are a scream!"

Duk Pin staggered down the mountain to safety. His ears tingled with frost-shtick, caused by hearing old jokes in cold weather. He recovered quickly and led a mission to rescue the nobleman. They found nothing, but heard horrifying laughter echo down the slopes.

"THAT'S A GOOD ONE, SIR PERCY! HEY, LET'S TAKE THIS SHOW ON THE ROAD!"